Emma's Rug

Allen Say

HOUGHTON MIFFLIN COMPANY BOSTON

Walter Lorraine *wl* Books

Library of Congress Cataloging-in-Publication Data

Say, Allen.
   Emma's rug / Allen Say.
       p. cm.
   Summary: A young artist finds that her creativity comes from
within when the rug that she had always relied upon for inspiration
is destroyed.
   RNF ISBN 0-395-74294-3   PA ISBN 0-618-33523-4
   [1. Creativity — Fiction. 2. Rugs — Fiction. 3. Drawing — Fiction.]
I. Title
PZ7.S2744Em 1996
[E] — dc20   96-14189
                                                                 CIP
                                                                  AC

Printed in Singapore by Tien Wah Press (Pte) Ltd
TWP   20 19 18 17 16 15 14 13 12 11

To Frances and Leo

When Emma was born, someone gave her a rug.
It was a small rug, shaggy and plain, the
kind that keeps your feet warm in the bathroom.
So Mother laid it by the crib,
for the day the baby could stand on her feet.
And by the time Emma climbed out of the
crib by herself, no one remembered who
had given her the rug.

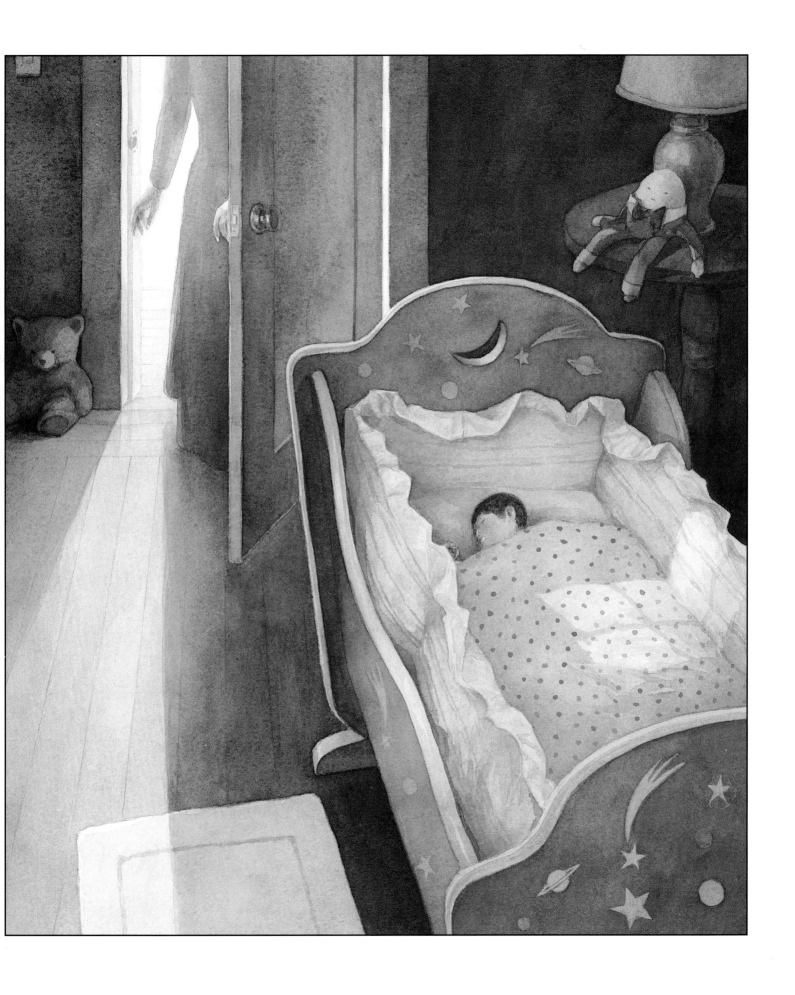

Emma loved the rug.
She lay on it and sat on it and she was happy.
When she began to walk, she carried it
everywhere she went, but never stepped on it.
Now she only stared at it, sitting
perfectly still, for long periods of time.
"That's not a blanket. It's her television,"
Father said.
"What do you see in that fuzzy thing?"
Mother asked.
Emma did not answer.

Before long, Emma began to draw and paint.
Her parents were quite impressed.
"Now, there is a wart hog,"
Father would say.
"Where did she see a pangolin? Is that
a tapir?" Mother would ask.
One weekend, Father put up a small drawing
table in the kitchen, and right away
the kitchen became Emma's favorite
place in the house.

On her first day at the kindergarten Emma
went straight up to an easel and began
to paint. Other children gathered around
and watched her wave the long brush like
a maestro's baton.
The grown-ups were amazed.
"She's special, that one,"
one adult said to another.

11

In the first grade, Emma won the top prize
in the art competition.
"What talent!" exclaimed the teacher.
"How do you know what to draw?" the children
asked. "Where do you get your ideas?"
"I just copy," Emma told them.
No one believed her.

Emma won more prizes.
Every time she entered a competition, she
received an award. Sometimes it was a ribbon,
other times a plaque or a trophy.
Her room became filled with awards.
Her parents were very proud.
But Emma only looked at her rug,
which she now kept hidden in the bottom
of her chest of drawers.
"What should I draw next?"
Emma asked every day.

Early one morning the telephone rang.
It was the mayor, asking to speak to Emma.
Mother thought it was a prank, but
then she recognized the voice, which she had
heard on television many times.
"Congratulations!" the mayor announced.
"Your daughter has won first prize in our
annual citywide art competition. I am
sending a limousine at three-thirty today.
The reception is at the Museum of Art.
Please be ready."

At the reception many famous people
stared at Emma.
"She's so small!"
"What a doll!"
"Big talent in such a little thing!"
"How can she hold a brush in that hand?"
People cooed as cameras flashed. The mayor
presented her the winner's certificate
in a big frame.
"So how does it feel to be a celebrity?"
a newspaper reporter bent down to ask.
Emma didn't say a word.

The following morning, Mother went into
Emma's room. She frowned at the unmade bed.
Then she saw the rug, with the framed
certificate on top.
"Goodness' sakes, I don't think this thing
has ever been cleaned." Wiggling her nose,
she took the rug downstairs and put
it in the washing machine.

When Emma came home, she went to her room
and stared in the empty drawer.
She dashed into the kitchen and said,
"Where's my rug?"
"Oh, I washed it. It must be dry by now,"
Mother told her.
"You washed my rug?" Emma charged downstairs.
The rug had shriveled. It was ragged. All
the fluff was gone. It was very, very clean.
Emma cried out.

Next day at school, Emma didn't draw or paint.
She never opened her mouth, and her hands
didn't come out of her pockets.
"Do you feel all right?" the teacher asked.
Emma only nodded.
"You can use my crayons," Alex offered.
Emma pushed the box away.
Days went by. Emma didn't speak, and soon
the children ignored her. After a while,
it was as if she weren't there anymore.

Emma took down all the drawings and paintings
from the walls of her room. She put
the prize ribbons and plaques and trophies
and medals into cardboard boxes.
She gathered up her colors and pencils and
brushes. Then she took them all down to
the garage and stuffed them in the trash bin.
The last thing she threw away was her rug.
"There," she said. "Kid stuff."

All afternoon Emma sat in her empty room.
It seemed somehow larger and brighter.
"No more pictures," Emma murmured.
Then something made her jump. From the
corner of her eye she thought she saw
something move behind her. She knew there
was only the wall there, all bare now, yet
she turned — as if to catch sight
of something flying away.
She gave a cry.

Emma rushed outside.

"It can't be!" she said, breathing faster.

She saw the eyes watching her and then

the faces of creatures all around.

She knew them from before.

She had thought she would never see again.

"I can see you!" Emma cried with joy.

The trees rustled, as if laughing.

And then it was quiet.